WITCH HEARTS

MAGIC AND MAGE SERIES - EPISODE 1

ANGHARAD THOMPSON REES

To you, dear reader.
May you find your own inner magic…

SISTERS OF THREE

The three sisters peered through the crack of the door, cringing when the old wood creaked. Breath held, they squinted to better see into the darkened room. Moonlight spread from a tiny window, casting its blue glow over a motionless silhouette.

"She's getting worse," Morganne said, watching their mother lay motionless, her breathing so light she hardly made a sound. Morganne closed the door, and her eyes, to stop her younger sisters seeing her tears.

"Maybe the doctor was wrong, maybe there is something we can do?" Fae asked in a whisper of a voice like soft wind parting grass. Fae—youngest sister, though only by several hours. But triplets always cling to the important fact of who was born first.

Morganne, Amara, and Fae. That's the order they were born and the order in which their mother addressed them, though she hadn't for weeks. And the girls began to wonder if she ever would again. The peculiar malady had rendered her still and silent, and all the more unnerving considering their mother had been as strong as a carthorse.

Amara, middle sister and thus the quietest, stared out the cabin's window searching for answers within the darkness. Dawn lined the horizon, but the sky was still inky blue, and the full moon hovered low and wide. It cast shadows and blue light across their small garden and the woods beyond. The dark soothed Amara, perhaps because the midnight sky matched her ebony hair and cobalt eyes as dark as the universe itself. But it was the moon she gazed at now, the low and heavy full moon that always seemed to speak to her, whisper secrets, grant her ideas—though she would never admit it, especially knowing what village girls whispered about the three sisters between cupped hands and narrowing eyes.

People thought sisters of three were strange—and strange often equated to unusual, and unusual was open to gossip, and tales, and untruths; which was to say, rumors.

"Quiet One," Morganne said, wrapping an arm around Amara's shoulder. "What are you thinking? Your thoughts are always so deep and brooding."

Amara's lips formed a tight line, a half attempt at a false smile. "Our mother is dying, sister. Deep and brooding seems the correct way to think."

Fae moved toward her older sisters, her footsteps light like a spring cloud, her voice lighter still. "But you always come up with the best ideas when you stare at the full moon."

Yes, that she did. But it was yet another reason to let her thoughts remain silent, like a river running under a vast mountain. Flowing, always flowing, but secret and unseen, certainly unheard. A secret she kept for herself.

A loud mewl sounded in the stillness of their thoughts and grabbed the girls' attention. Shadow, their cat—as black as coal and bad dreams—stared in through the window from his usual spot on the flower box.

"Oh Shadow, Mother would kill you if she saw you sitting there squashing the Chrysanthemums," Morganne said as she opened the window to let him in. But he rose and stared at her in the way only a cat can, refusing to enter and instead, Shadow turned away. He flicked his tail high over his back like a royal command, and graciously descended from the window box to the garden below. He trotted along the garden path like a king, stopping twice to look over his shoulder as the girls watched.

"We had better get our cloaks," Amara said, smoothing her thick black curls in preparation for a journey. She turned to her eldest sister, wiping away a remaining tear she spied stuck on Morganne's lower lashes. Amara, as dark as night, attempted a smile. "We need to follow Shadow."

"I thought you'd say that," Fae said like a rainbow in a summer shower—slightly hopeful, slightly sad.

"But the sun shan't rise for hours," Morganne began, the voice of reason that often comes with being the eldest. "We've not tended a fire for Mother, or prepared the broth..." She stopped when she noticed Amara gazing at the full moon again.

"I have a feeling, dear sisters," Amara began, as grave as a forgotten cemetery. "That if we do not follow Shadow into the woods, we shall soon have no mother to tend."

Yes, Amara always had her best ideas under the full moon, and neither Morganne nor Fae would ignore her. Fae had already donned her grey cloak, the hood all but covering her long, flowing locks of winter sunshine. She held her sisters' belongings aloft.

"Onwards," Fae said, with a lightness of a hopeful springtime breeze, and the three sisters stepped into the night.

2

INTO THE WOODS

*S*hadow sauntered ahead, slipping between light and dark. He did not follow the well-beaten path meandering through the woods, and instead curled his way around trees and undergrowth. The three sisters followed, early morning dew from overgrown shrubs and branches dampening the hems of their cloaks.

"We should not wander far from the path," Morganne said. Eldest. Voice of reason. Sensible.

"Shhh," whispered Fae. Youngest. Voice of light and air. Inquisitive.

"We follow Shadow," said Amara. Middle child. Voice older than time. Resolute.

Shards of the moon's light penetrated the gloom,

highlighting thorny brambles and night-time animals going about their business. It enabled the girls to see where they were going as they traipsed deeper into the woods than ever before.

"I'm only saying," said Morganne, peeping over her shoulder thrice, ignoring the play of shadows casting dark shapes amongst the trees, "that we've all heard the rumors about this forest. I'm not one for superstition but something is wrong—*strange* wrong."

Amara agreed, but continued regardless, despite a peculiar sense within her bones. It was not a chill, but a heaviness lingering in the spaces where her joints ended and blood flowed—and it pulsed now in double-time to a worrisome rhythm. Amara pushed it aside, along with a heavy branch blocking their way.

"Sister?" Fae questioned, her footsteps slowing.

"I know it's dangerous, but we have but one chance to save Mother. No ordinary remedy has helped—the doctor has all but given up. We need to find a herb to help, and we need to find it tonight," Amara said. She looked at the moon with a furrowed brow.

Fae nodded, her ocean-blue eyes searching into forgotten memories. "Yes, I remember reading about such a herb... Witch Hazel, a cure all for unnamed afflictions."

Morganne gulped, knowing the Witch Hazel's healing properties die with the waning moon. Tonight *was* their last chance. Tomorrow, the full moon would diminish, and with it the Witch Hazel's power.

They clambered over rotten logs, their hems catching and tearing on thorns and brambles. About their feet, small forest creatures of the night scurried about their business in haste before the morning light. Owls hooted, rats squeaked, and somewhere, far in the distance, a lone wolf howled.

The three sisters stopped, as did the swishing of grass and shrubs around them. No animals flitted now.

Silence.

Stillness.

"The lone wolf's cry," Fae said, her voice a threatening summer storm, with eyes as wide as the low full moon. Fae's heart thumped into the silence of the night.

"We must find the Witch Hazel and get back immediately," Morganne agreed. "Not that I believe the superstitious nonsense about—"

Amara cut in, reciting the old tune the villagers taught their children as soon as they were old enough to understand the power of folktales and legends.

"When the lone wolf cries

Before the night dies
And the forest sings
Of night-time things
And the sun and moon meet in the sky
The time has come for you to——"

"Poppycock!" Morganne called, though a shiver ran from the base of her spine to the crown of her red-tipped curls. "It's a childish tale to scare children into staying tucked up in their beds at night." The quiver in her voice exposed the lie of confidence in her words, and she looked around, noticing the sun on the horizon, the moon not quite ready to dip. She bit her bottom lip to stop it from trembling.

"What do we do now?" asked Fae, timid.

Amara hugged her sisters both then spoke the truth. "I don't know. Shadow has disappeared—that cat! Perhaps he has left us in the right place to discover the herb?"

They smiled then; perhaps Amara was right. Perhaps the cat could be trusted—difficult as it may be to trust a cat wholeheartedly—and they went about, rummaging around the dew-drenched ferns with their pale, cold hands.

The lone wolf called once more. The sun rose and cast its golden shards of light across the forest loam.

The moon tipped its hat, meeting the sun in a perfect line above the horizon. A shiver spread through Amara's bones, and her heart beat once more to the tune of 'something is wrong.'

A branch snapped underfoot behind them.

3

A PRETTY PENNY

"Got'cha!" growled a gruff voice.

A net whipped through the air, bundling the three sisters together and catapulting them high into the trees.

"We've gor'em, Boris! We've captured them witches!" cried a hunchbacked man. He giggled and dribbled beneath the trap filled with the struggling sisters, rubbing his hands together with greed and mirth.

From behind a great oak, a hooded man emerged, his features hidden by shadow and his thick hessian cloak. Though he wore the habit of a priest, the sisters could easily see he was no such thing. A wickedness seeped from each step he took, crunching upon dried leaves and fallen branches like broken promises.

"Very good, Cuthbert. Very good indeed." The hooded man looked upwards, and the three sisters—as different as three seasons—stared down. "Winch them down, Cuthbert, my old friend. I'll prepare the cage."

The hunchback obliged, loosening the ropes and allowing the net to fall with a jolt. Cuthbert yanked it to an abrupt halt just before it hit the ground, and it swayed in mid-air like a violent storm. The sisters gasped, wide-eyed, but said not a word.

"Little witchies!" The hunchback giggled, peering up at them.

Fae glared at her sisters, her brow a knot of confusion, "Witches?" she whispered.

Morganne reached for her youngest sister's hand, and in soft soothing whisper said, "it's a stupid mistake, they'll soon see."

Amara said nothing, and instead glared at the hooded man as he readied a botched-together wooden cage set precariously atop a rotten cart. Three horses stood ahead of the dilapidated carriage, solemn and waiting, heavy headed and lifeless. Long shaft poles attached to their sides penned them one behind the other. Amara's gaze skimmed over the horses' protruding hips and ribs, and she felt an emptiness in the pit of her own stomach with the shallowness of the beasts' tucked skeletal frames.

"Look 'ere!" The hunchback said, almost jumping on the spot with delight. He let go of the rope and the net crashed to the floor. Fae sobbed and Morganne put a reassuring arm around her sister's shoulder that did nothing to reassure either of them.

"Our witches be like our 'orses. A black one, a white one, an' a red one!"

"Shut up, you moronic imbecile," the hooded man spat.

Cuthbert silenced, the smile twisting and draining from his face like dirty water down a plug hole. He stepped back, cowering slightly. A horse snorted.

"The peculiar thing is not that they match our good-for-nothing cart horses," though he stopped to admire the comparison—Morganne with curls that looked like flickering flames, Amara with her midnight-sky locks, and Fae's white blonde hair that looked like winter's first frost. "No, the peculiar thing it that the witches, despite the obvious hair differences, are identical."

Cuthbert snorted a nervous laugh, not truly sure if this was the correct reaction his master expected from him.

"We're triplets, sir," Morganne said in the bravest voice she could muster. "And we are not witches at all, we were simply in the woods looking for some...

oomph!" Morganne rubbed her side and scowled at Amara, who ever so slightly shook her head, warning eyes spelling a 'no.'

Of course, Morganne thought. *If I was to say we were looking for herbs this man will definitely believe us to be such terrible things as witches.*

"...For our cat," Amara continued. "We have lost our cat, that's what we were looking for out here."

The hooded man wagged a finger at them and in a mockingly-sweet voice said, "You won't speak another word, little witches, and if I find your cat you can only guess what my old friend here would do."

The hooded man nodded towards Cuthbert and made a gesture with his forefinger across his throat. The hunchback laughed fiendishly.

"Load them up, Cuthbert. The Witch Hunter General will pay a pretty penny for this collection." Then, watching the hunchback load the girls into the cage said, "it's off to the witch trials for you."

The sisters huddled into each other, shivering and trying not to sob as the lock on the cage was set. They had failed to find the herb. They had failed to help their mother. And now, as the hunchback sent a whip slicing through the air to rouse the pathetic-looking horses forward, they had failed in any way possible to escape their fate.

"Perhaps the story about the lone wolf's cry is true," whispered Fae as sadly as a late autumn breeze stripping the last leaf from a tree.

Nobody had the hope to disagree.

4

RED

The cart rolled and clattered along cobblestones, swaying with groans and protests from the hobbled-together wood—the cage containing the three sisters altogether too heavy to be placed upon such a vehicle. Several times it looked to topple but righted itself when the cargo inside shifted and shunted with squeaks and squeals.

"What will happen when we get to the trial?" asked Fae.

Nobody answered.

Amara continued to stare at the moon dipping below the horizon, and watched clouds forming high in the sky. They swirled around confused and angry, like her dark and foreboding mood. She nibbled her already bitten down nails.

"Looks like snow," Cuthbert, the hunchback said, craning his neck to look over his shoulder. It should not snow, not in spring at least. He cast a nervous glance at the three sisters and smiled meekly, which soon morphed into a grimace. "Aye, this ain't your doing, is it?"

"Don't encourage them," the hooded man said in a bored tone. "If you're going to do any encouraging, encourage these good-for-nothing beasts forward to the witch trial. These horses are as lazy as a May Fly in June, and the quicker we get there, the quicker we get our coin."

A long driving whip sliced through the air, cracking upon the hides of the horses, and the cart lurched forward. One horse—the red one, they didn't have names—stumbled, and got a second crack for its audacity. The hooded man growled, and unheard by the humans, the horses talked amongst themselves, their voices as silent as the sisters' deepest fears...

I haven't the strength to keep going, cried Red in the minds of his companions. His unshod and bruised hooves pounded the ground, feeling every stone and uneven surface through his thin soles. Pain shot up his legs as if his bones were burning hot pokers, though his stumbles only served to encourage his masters to drive them forward all the more.

We have to keep going, said White. *Perhaps when we get to town, there'll be a stable with warm golden straw and fresh meadow hay.*

Black snorted and tossed his head. *You're dreaming,* he said, out of breath. *When have we ever had such a thing?*

But the prison wardens will get lots of coin for three witches —they could afford to buy us some decent food and shelter for a change, said White in a desperately hopeful way.

They'll spend it on beer and frivolity, White, while we wait outside tired and cold.

There was so much truth in the statement that the horses spoke no more. They carried on, regardless. A prison warden's set of horses was a very sorry sight, and each one had the scars to prove it. On they trotted, while flakes of snow fell and nestled onto their dull, coarse coats, or tangled within their matted manes. On they duly continued, though the wooden shafts of the cart rubbed their protruding hip bones red raw. And on they journeyed, regardless of their balding and itchy skin beneath their unwashed bridles, where dried sweat built up and acted as blunt razors upon their faces.

I can't... Red cried, and stumbled again, this time falling to his knees with a crash. The cart shuddered to a halt, pulling both White and Black by the metal bit in their mouths.

They reared and called out.

Red?!

The cage toppled.

The three sisters screamed.

The hunchback and the hooded man growled while Red lay sprawled on the cold, stony ground, blood staining the snow crimson.

THE PRICE OF WATER

The three sisters huddled into one another, the cage splintered around them.

"Are we all okay?" Morganne whispered.

Fae sniffed and nodded, casting a timid glance at the men before her. Amara did not attempt a reply, instead, she stared at the poor red horse sprawled on the road; watched its blood stain the pristine snow with red. The other two horses pawed at the ground, fractious, the cart tilting upwards behind them. A wheel continued to spin in mid-air.

"Get that lazy, good-for-nothing horse up from the ground, Cuthbert," growled the hooded man. "I'll muster up these witches so they don't run off, we need to get back on the road. Don't want to miss today's trial."

The hooded man's presence was deterrent enough to stop the three sisters from running away. He was tall, taller than most men, but it wasn't his height or broadness of shoulder or the way his features hid within the shadows of the hood that scared them. It was the aura leaking from him—black as death and cold as fear. Besides, there was nowhere *to* run; the land was empty and barren and white for miles around. They were nowhere, an in-between place where villages did not meet and towns a distant memory.

Fae whimpered—a chill sound like sudden frost. Morganne gritted her teeth. But Amara, Amara found the quiet place within her brewing like a storm as she watched the hunchback kick the horse's rump in an attempt to rouse it.

"The horse needs water," she called out, as spitefully as frostbite. "They all do."

The hunchback stopped and glared at the dark-haired triplet. His hands fumbled with a loose button on his stained black cloak. A nervous gesture.

"See that," cried the hooded man. "See that, Cuthbert. Proof she can talk to animals! She must burn at the stake, it's not normal nor right—"

"You don't need magical powers to know these poor horses are thirsty, look at them," Amara said, her usual calm rattled. "Pinched stomachs, dry eyes—a good feed would help, too, if those ribs are any thing to go by."

The hooded man didn't look toward the horses, but he did step away from the girls, thoughtful.

"Perhaps," he mumbled more to himself than anyone else. "They have been on the road for days and I can't remember the last stop for a rest. Lazy, good-for-nothing beasts." He strode away from the three sisters, content in their fear to stay put, and walked to the cart. It still lay askew and Cuthbert hovered around an unhinged wheel, trying to work out how to mount it in place. The hooded man, however, reached past the hunchback and grabbed a small wooden bucket from the back of the cart. Striding back to the three sisters, he thrust the pail into Amara's chest.

"Here, if you're so concerned about my nags, you can give them water yourself—only *you* mind, don't want you all coming up with grand and ridiculous plots to escape."

He grabbed Amara by her hair and pulled her up. She scrunched her face, gulping down her pain and biting her tongue so she neither yelped nor whimpered as the roots of her black hair tugged at her cold scalp— she did not want to give him the satisfaction. The hooded man pulled her to the far side of the cart, gripping her shoulder in a clenching vice.

Beside the cart was a spindly riverbank that ran the length of the now snow-laden road into the bleak horizon. Its gentle trickle lost in the steepness of its banks and the vast and empty countryside—a nothingness under a frigid blanket of white.

"Go on," the hooded man commanded, shoving Amara with such force she nearly fell to her knees. "Get yourself down there and get the nags some water, no more than a bucket each, mind. The stupid beasts will colic."

She gulped, the steepness and deepness of the bank causing her to sway—a mild vertigo that ceased immediately when the chestnut horse beside her groaned with exhaustion. A second horse neighed with a feeble whinny, though Amara could not be sure which one for she was already scrambling down the slippery slope, descending into the darkness. Amara slipped, losing her footing and slid over brambles and past several small, crooked trees. The dirty bucket tumbled ahead of her, not looking to stop.

"Stupid girl," Amara cursed aloud, grasping onto a thorny branch. She managed to stop herself from tumbling and swore beneath her breath again, this time at the crimson dots forming on her cold palms. She wiped them on her cloak, red trails like tears on the wet, grey cotton. With a breath, she scuttled downwards on her bottom, grasping at nearby vines and brambles as she followed the bucket's path.

Finally, Amara reached the freezing water, gasping at the coldness of melting snow underfoot. A wicked wind danced around her ankles causing her to shiver, and her cloak, soaked through, seeped a deeper coldness and damp onto her thin nightdress that now clung to her skin. Her fingertips dipped into the ice-cold water with the bucket and she sucked in air between chattering teeth—her heart pausing with shock for several beats. Yet somehow, she suddenly felt alive; to feel the cold so wholly. She hoped the water would do the same for the poor horses.

Climbing back up the hill was an equally arduous task, a semi-crawl on feet and hands, water sloshing from the bucket as Amara slipped and slithered, losing her footing. All the while she thought of her sisters, and her mother laying in a cold bed with no fire to warm her, no herbs to heal her. She thought of the witch trials and all the innocent women and children who came before her, just to line the pockets of the infamous Witch Hunter General. The witch trial had nothing to do with magic and everything to do with power; the power of gold coins.

Finally, Amara reached the summit, her cheeks flush with cold and effort. She offered the first bucket of water to the red horse breathing heavily on the ground.

"Here," said Amara, taking the bucket to the horse's mouth. She smoothed his neck, noting the flaky skin and scurvy coat. She shook her head, her heart heavy, while the horse took deep drafts of water. Amara went to the roadside lowering to her hands and knees, moving armfuls of snow. She ignored the biting pain it caused, and collected handfuls of grass from beneath the frozen blanket. She offered some to the poor red horse.

Thank you, said Red into Amara's mind as he chomped feverishly on the grass.

Amara recoiled, hands rising to cover her gaping mouth.

Thank you, for I fear I would have died of thirst and starvation if it weren't for you, Red continued between ravenous chomps.

"What? What's happening? How can you speak?" Amara said, and looked around to check her captors were not listening. They weren't.

Horses always speak, humans just don't always hear us, said White as Red rose to stand. He shook his body and Amara backed away, shocked. *I guess you hear us because you're not human, you're a witch.*

"I am no such thing!" cried Amara, and she took

the empty bucket from Red and ran. She bolted back down the hill to fetch more water—an excuse to get some space; thoughts whirling, words hurtling.

I am not a witch, she thought to herself, over and over as she scrambled to the freezing water to refill the bucket.

I am not a witch, she repeated as she watched the water sail past her like her old thoughts and denials.

I'm not a witch... a pause, a recollection of thoughts —a question. *Am I?*

Above Amara, lightning crackled in the snow-filled sky, reflecting off the dancing snowflakes landing like stars in her midnight hair.

HOPE

*H*ours passed, and Amara—middle sister, quiet, deep—said not a word. She stared out at the changing landscape from the botched-up cage on the botched-up cart, trying to ignore the fact that the little red horse had spoken to her, trying to ignore the thunderclouds rumbling above her head in the low sky. It matched her mood, as the snow had, and she was beginning to wonder if that was merely a coincidence or not. She wondered about the *funny feelings* in her bones, and the good ideas she received when staring at the moon.

"Sister?" Fae asked, a whisper of wind. "You are still pale, paler even. Won't you tell us what happened out there, at the river?"

"Hush, little sister," cooed Morganne. "Amara will

speak when she is ready, as she always does." She smiled tightly and squeezed Amara's cold hand.

Amara pulled away. "It's all my fault," she said, as quiet as the flurrying snow.

"No," Morganne said, reaching for her hand again and clasping it harder.

"It was *I* who led you into the heart of the forest—"

"No," said Fae, "it was Shadow, our cat."

"Shut up back there," the hooded man yelled, and Morganne and Fae obeyed. And although Amara appeared to follow his orders, it wasn't the case, for truly, she was deep in thought, deep in wonder, and more than anything else, deep in denial.

Sated, slightly, the horses continued their trek. Their heads hung low and hooves dragged, leaving long marks in the snow. A bucket of water and a handful of frozen grass only goes so far after all. But Red, Red had a little more bounce in his walk, his ears a little more pricked forward, eyes a little brighter.

All this time we've been carting so-called witches to trial, and this is the first time we've ever carried a real witch! Red mused.

Black said nothing, but White twitched an ear.

Do you think they are evil, like all the people say? asked White.

Red shook his head, his scraggly mane shivered. *How can they be? It was the witch who gave us water, gathered frozen grass with her bare hands.*

Black snorted, breath from his nostrils warming the air like a stream of dragon smoke. *If the witch could help, she'd help herself. And she can't even do that. Why humans fear them, I don't know. They are as powerless as we are.*

He snorted again, which usually meant the end of conversation. But Red couldn't stop the wonderings in his mind, curling and uncurling.

I think she'll help us, said Red. *If we help them first.*

Nonsense, Red, said Black, and he swished his dull, knotted tail.

White, forever hopeful, pranced a little. *I agree with you, Red, though I don't know how we can help.*

Red also pranced a happy dance, though stopped abruptly when a sharpness pulled at his mouth. *Ouch!* he whinnied, and the coachmen growled at him. Red swished his head and continued. *Did you see how easily hindered this cart became when I stumbled?*

Black neighed in agreement.

What if, instead of stopping the cart, we all galloped off, in different directions at the same time?

Black stamped a hoof. *What about it? Even if we do,*

it's impossible—our masters will only capture us and punish us all the more!

There was a pause, a silence of muted hoofbeats on snow and creaking wood as the cart rolled along.

It could *work,* White said in the merest of whispers.

No, said Black. *It could not.*

It might *work,* said Red with a bit of cheer.

But it might not... Black quickly replied.

How do you know if you won't even try? asked Red, trumping the argument. *I'd rather try with a bit of hope than never try at all.*

Again, muted hoof falls. Deep thoughts. Twirling snow and a voice, a tiny voice in the back of the horses' minds.

I can hear you, thought Amara into their minds, her voice tremulous. *I can hear everything you say.*

The horses startled, spooking in a way that made the cart lurch and creak. The coachmen growled, nervous.

Red whinnied.

Amara continued. *And I* will *help, if I can... if you can first free us.*

What do you think, Black? asked White.

The muddied black horse broke into a frenzied gallop.

7

THE POWER OF THREE

The cart rose into the air then slammed to the ground with a deafening shudder. On the horses galloped, ignoring the pain in their mouths as the coachman yanked the reins and swore. Two girls cried out. One did not, and the smallest sunbeam penetrated the snow clouds, shining down towards her and lighting her thick ebony curls.

"What's gotten into these bleedin' nags?" Cuthbert said, clinging to the reins with all his might.

"This," the hooded man began before toppling backwards, then righting himself. "This is what happens when you allow your nags to be well fed and watered."

The cart groaned, protesting at the speed as it darted along the rutted track. The wheels rattled. The cart rocked, threatening to topple. The horses galloped faster.

"I'm scared," whimpered Fae, clinging to her sisters both.

Amara took a lock of her sister's white hair and twirled it around her fingers. "Do not be scared." She dared a smile in the chaos. "The horses will free us."

Fae smiled but Morganne shot a dark look. "You shouldn't say things like that, you shouldn't say things that aren't true," Morganne said.

The elder and middle sisters shared a look full of unspoken truths—thoughts, fears, ideas, disbelief.

The cart rolled forward, bounding and bouncing along the cobbled lane at speed, closer and closer to the witch trials—the landscape a blur of white, white snow. The coachmen hollered. The horses screeched. Two sisters cried, while the third closed her eyes and concentrated...

After three, Amara thought to the horses.

Ready, said Red.

On your count, said White.

Black said nothing, but duly galloped forward.

They sped over a small stone bridge, an ice blue

river running beneath. The horses' hooves clattered and clanged, slipping against cobblestones buried beneath the snow.

"Darn these good-for-nothing—" A deafening crack stopped the hooded man's words. The cart dropped to the left with a crash, the wheel rolling past them. The horses continued, sparks flying from the cart as it scraped along the ground.

Amara took a breath, and counted.

One... Snow flurried harder, dancing on a wind whipping from the north.

Two... A murder of crows broke from a snow-laden oak tree, cawing into the air like billowing black smoke.

Three... Three horses parted. Three sisters fell. Three seconds of eerie stillness.

8

PARTING

The sisters lay sprawled on the snow, their wet cloaks askew, their breathing heavy. Stillness.

No cart scraping along the ground. No galloping hoofbeats. No screaming and hollering men. Just silence, and the delicate fall of snowflakes on cold skin.

The horses stopped. Stunned, turning to take in the carnage they'd created. Red stamped a hoof. Amara rose to her feet. The girl and horse locked eyes across the void, and Amara felt she could see the entire universe in those large, black orbs. A shuffling, a shadow, moving from the corner of her eye caused Amara to break their gaze. The hooded man crawled from the ruined cart, his hood fallen back to reveal his twisted features.

Amara gasped as his milk-white eyes stared into her soul. The entire left side of his face looked to melt towards his neck, flesh and gore singed to expose pockets of bone and teeth. He had no lips, just a cavernous hole that morphed into an angry smile. Rising to his feet, Boris did not attempt to look away nor hide his hideously-scarred and misshapen head now it was exposed.

"B-Boris," Cuthbert whispered, as he scrambled to his hands and knees. "Your 'ood. It's come off your f-face." There was terror in that voice, a tremulous stutter, a disbelief.

"I don't give a monkey's aunt about my hood, Cuthbert." Then he raised his voice and grew in stature, in awfulness. "I care about what these witches are capable of doing." He patted his sticky cheek with tender fingers, exposing the truth that his hatred for witches burrowed deeper than the scars upon his face. "I made a promise not to let these awful creatures walk the earth. Now, *get the witches!*"

His words ignited Amara. She grabbed at her sisters, pulling them from their stunned heaps on the ground. "Come sisters, we must run. We must run for our lives!"

Grabbing hold of Fae's trembling hands, she pulled her toward the horses.

"Where will we go?" cried Fae, her voice a hopeless leaf in the hurricane's winds.

"We head for the horses." Amara turned, "Morganne, keep up!"

But Morganne hobbled then collapsed to the ground. She cried out. "My ankle, I've hurt my ankle when the cage fell." Morganne bit back a sob as Boris and Cuthbert stalked toward them.

Amara turned to Fae. "The horses are coming for us. Run to them and mount whichever one you get to first." She ran back toward her sister who clutched her ankle and writhed in pain. And then in her mind, Amara roared to the horses.

Now!

The horses turned and galloped toward them, sending clots of snow flying into the freezing air. Fae ran like the wind to meet them, hood fallen back, blond hair trailing behind her. Morganne struggled to her feet. Amara panicked, torn between helping each sister. The men stalked closer to Morganne.

"Red!" Amara cried. "I need you! I need your help, now!"

The red horse galloped to their side. Amara took Morganne by the shoulders. "I'm going to leg you up onto Red... and it's going to hurt your ankle."

Morganne nodded, biting back a sob, but she didn't

attempt to wipe away the tears trailing down her cheeks.

"After three?" Amara asked.

Morganne turned, grabbing hold of the scraggly red mane at the horse's withers. She stood on her good leg and lifted her injured foot for a leg up.

"One, two," Amara began, and Morganne held her breath, bracing herself. "Three!"

Morganne screamed out, a harrowing sound that echoed across the valley and vibrated in the core of the world. She collapsed onto Red's skeletal back, doubling over the horse's neck in sobs of pain.

"Go," screamed Amara. Red didn't wait to reply, and galloped into the distance.

"*You* won't get away so easily," snarled Boris, stalking toward her. He saw his own putrid reflection in her stunned-wide emerald eyes—the flaking flesh, the exposed left eye socket—but any disgust he felt ebbed with the relish her fear conjured within him.

Amara backed away, one slow step at a time. Boris paced forwards, a lion ready to pounce.

Where are the other horses? Amara thought to herself.

Boris reached for her, but she was paralyzed with fear. Amara watched his ruined face, seeing him and only him. There was a thrumming. Quick and fast. *My heart? My bones?*

A flash of black. A flick of a tail.

No, she realized as withered hands reached closer to her. *My escape.*

Quickly! said Black. *I dare not stop, he'll grab us both. You'll have to mount me as I gallop by.*

Amara readied herself, steadying her pounding heart. The now un-hooded man growled. Black screeched a high-pitched neigh into the pale white sky, and as the horse whirled by, galloping in a tight circle around the girl—*the witch*—Amara grabbed a tangled mass of black mane. The horse spun. Amara used the momentum to launch herself onto the horse's back. And as quickly as that, they galloped away from the un-hooded man and the witch trial.

"We did it!" Amara screamed, heart fit to burst with fear and relief and excitement. They galloped towards Red and Morganne in the far distance. "We did it!"

She reveled in her freedom. Cold wind sliced against her cheeks as the thrumming hooves pounded the soft carpet of snow. Her hair, loose and wild, billowed around her, ebony curls dancing like Black's mane. So much ground they covered.

We'll be home before the sun sets and the day is done, thought Amara with relief. But her smile waned like a sliver of an old moon. Why then, if they had escaped, did her blood suddenly start pumping with the beat of 'something is wrong?'

"Oh no…" she whispered.

And Black shrieked a blood curdling call.

Amara turned her head as Black slowed and spun on her haunches—sharp and quick.

And there, they watched—dread and disbelief seeping through their veins like the cold, wet snow upon their skin.

The hunchback grabbed White's reins, pulling sharply at the metal bit in her mouth. And bundled in the un-hooded man's clutches, Fae screamed.

THE TRUTH

*A*mara stared open mouthed, while tears streamed down her cheeks blushed red from cold and shame. Muted hoof falls hastened towards her.

"Oh Amara," Morganne said, gasping with a deeper pain than her throbbing ankle. "What can we do?"

Amara said not a word. There was no moon to speak to her. She had no answers.

Beneath the sisters, the horses heaved with labored breaths, having not exerted themselves in such a way for years. They quivered on fatigued legs, breath fogging the frigid air around them. Sweat rose from the horses' bodies, swirling mist surrounding them in a deep gloom of failure.

We must go back, panted Red.

And how can we get back to them? Black said with a shake of her head. *I can barely breathe, and look at your knees.*

At this, Amara looked over at the little red horse. The cuts on his knees from his earlier stumble gaped— the soft tissue around them swollen and sore. Droplets of blood trailed down his slender legs and dotted upon the snow-laden ground. Red said nothing, and took an ailed step forward. His head shooting up with pain as he did so.

"I'll get off and lead the him," Morganne suggested, following Amara's gaze. "I didn't realize the horse was lame."

"And how will you lead him? You're as lame as Red," Amara said, trying to keep the rising panic from spilling out as anger. She shook her head. "This is all my fault." Hot tears stung her cold, cold cheeks.

"No, it's nobody's fault but those greedy, horrid men stealing away innocent girls in the dead of night," Morganne said. She reached out a hand to her younger sister but stopped with the darkness of Amara's brooding stare.

Overhead, a clap of thunder rumbled and groaned, chasing the forming dark clouds with fury. Amara looked up, feeling the storm welling within her.

No, she *was* the storm and somehow, it raged within her and *from* her. Lightning split the sky in two—a sharp line of jagged teeth gnawing at the grumbling clouds.

"It *is* my fault," Amara began again, her words roaring above the crashing thunder overhead. "It's my fault because, because..."

Morganne stared at Amara and saw nothing of the quiet and still middle sister anymore. She saw power and beauty and... truth.

Morganne broke a worried smile. "It's not your fault you're a witch, my beautiful sister," Morganne said. Eldest. Voice of reason. And Amara would have flung herself into her sister's embrace had they not been onboard the tired, panting horses.

"You... you know?" Amara asked, incredulous.

Morganne nodded, cautious.

"And you are not scared?"

Morganne smiled and shook her head, her red curls tumbling like flames.

I am a witch, Amara thought to herself. And then, aloud, she finally admitted the truth she'd known all along. "I *am* a witch, sister. And *I* am scared. Scared of who I am, scared that those men have Fae, and if anyone should be standing trial, it should be me, not our poor, innocent, and youngest sibling."

Silence. The sisters stared at one another as if the entire world hinged on the next words spoken.

It was Black's voice that broke into the terrified chamber of Amara's mind.

And are you not also innocent? he asked. *Should you be judged just because you are different?*

Should our differences not be celebrated? asked Red, soft as a spring morning.

"Do not be scared, darling sister. There is power in accepting ourselves for who we truly are. And who knows what that power may mean for you?"

Yes, thought Amara. She *was* different. Different in a good way. And now all she needed was to work out how to make *her* difference *make* a difference, and get her sister back. Amara dismounted, patting Black's sweat-lathered neck, the coarse hair sticky beneath her palm. She stood, face turned upwards toward the falling snow and raging clouds. With a deep breath, Amara sucked in the energy of the world, arms flung wide, embracing her new truth, feeling it tingle in every cell. She heard it whisper in the small place between the joints of her bones. And her blood sang, and it sang one word over and over and over again.

Magic.

10

MAGIC

The world no longer seemed white and muted. It was no longer bleak and lackluster. Instead, every thing glistened and pulsed with energy. Amara knew, deep down, she had been hiding the truth from herself her entire life; but now she believed it, and in turn, believed in herself.

The world around her morphed into a wonder of color and infinite possibilities. Wind touched her skin, yet it no longer felt like a breeze—it whispered, instead, of oceans travelled, mountains passed, streams and rivers of colors she had never before seen rippling beneath its touch. The ground beneath her feet no longer felt like something to simply stand upon. The rocks shared stories of far-off lands she was yet to visit, where the sun scorched the earth, and told

tales of the ancient forming of the world. Each
snowflake sang a song, stories of what it once was; ice
upon a white bear's frozen eyelash, or sea spray from a
voyaging ship discovering new horizons and lost hope.
And sadly, she felt every story the prison warden
horses had endured. She could taste their fear and
disappointment when she looked at the withered
beasts standing side-by-side. And she realized then, a
life lived under the control of another was no life
at all.

"Sister?" asked Morganne.

Morganne did not produce a story or song like the
world surrounding Amara did, and the young witch
reveled in the same constant, familiar blanket of love
Morganne always offered. Warm and safe. And as she
thought these things, golden sparks spread from Amara,
reaching out like a nebula explosion and shooting stars.
With gentle tendrils, the golden hue glittered and shimmered, surrounding her sister. Morganne shrieked, her
smile a happy confusion of surprise and delight.

"My ankle! My ankle no longer hurts!" Morganne
called, amazed within her globe of healing light.

The golden glitter grew like an expanding universe
of stars, to cover the little red horse. Red whickered,
tossing his head and swishing his tail, anxious with the
strange and otherworldly sensation.

It's okay, Amara spoke into the horse's mind. *I am trying to ease your pain.*

The warm glow spread to Red's gashed knees, blood trailed backwards from his hoof, cannon bone, and back to the slashes across his knees. The swelling lessened; the flesh healed. The horse snorted, a relaxed and contented sound.

It was a hypnotic feeling, to heal, and Amara swayed.

Careful, Red whispered. *You must not use too much power, you must protect your own energy.*

How do you know such things? Amara questioned within both her own and the horses' minds.

Because we are both beings of nature, said Red, and if a horse could smile, he would have done so in that moment.

She could feel how Red's heart now pumped stronger, how his hope blossomed with wellness, and Amara, despite Red's warning, could not help herself.

Breathing in energy from nature again, she flung her arms wide, calling the power of the wind, and the earth, and the faraway shore. Her hands pulsed, ice blue and gold swirling to form globes within her palms, and she flung the energy spheres toward both horses.

Like blue fire and glittering lightning, Amara's energy and love and hope reached out to the horses.

Swirling mists cascaded into one another like waterfalls and rainbows. And in an instant, the transformation took place.

The scraggly manes untangled and lengthened, leaving long, shining locks blowing and whipping in the wild winds. Dusty, dirty coats blossomed, flaky skin healing over protruding ribs that disappeared behind shimmering coats as the horses grew stronger, healthier. They seemed to double in size, such was their impressive stature. Black reared high and proud, boxing out her forelegs, muscles rippling.

Morganne, still sitting aboard Red, looked around in wonderment, both hands covering her wide smile.

"My gosh! What splendor!" Morganne said between giggles, the type of giggles that take place when one can not believe what one has seen. The horse beneath her gleamed, stamping a hoof and tossing his mane that looked like dancing flames.

She caught Amara's gaze. Locking stares. And Morganne was almost sure she saw her sister—her serious middle sister—*smirk*. Amara clicked her fingers and instantly, Morganne's damp, grey cape billowed around her, dancing like a giant boat sail in a high storm. The edges glittered, turning crimson. The hood shimmered, golden dust motes settling on the edges and trailing down the material that morphed into a deep, vibrant red like Morganne's own curls—and her horse's mane. A flickering flame in the white, white snow. Meanwhile, Amara's cloak became a midnight sky full of stars and moons dancing and twirling.

"And now," Amara said. "We rescue our sister."

She thrust her hands together over her head, a clap of thunder roaring as her palms met, and then she threw the storm towards the hooded man and his henchman, hoping it would slow them down, and ignoring the doubt forming in the pit of her stomach that her magic would not be enough to save her youngest sister.

11

A NEW RHYTHM

$\mathcal{I}$t mattered not how Fae screamed or wriggled or writhed. The men held her strong and true. Their fat, calloused fingers gripping into her fair, fair skin and making indents on her arms, already turning purple and bruised.

"Please," she called out like a delicate flower in a storm. "Please don't hurt me. Let me go!"

"Shut your trap and keep walking, witch!" The hunchback jeered, pulling on White's reins and bumping her gums with the sharp bit. He turned to the man with the scarred face and the pale white eyes. "Ain't that right, Boris?"

"Indeed, but keep control of that cursed, wretched nag." The man pulled his tattered hood back over his head, and his face disappeared in the shadows once more. He grabbed the reins from Cuthbert's hands while the white horse danced and shrieked around them, and shoved Fae into the hunchback's arms. "It does not matter that we lost the triplets. Now we have something even better..." he yanked the tough, dry reins, clanking the sharp metal bit harder against White's teeth and rubbed-raw gums. White screamed a high-pitched neigh and lowered her head. Submissive. "Now we have ourselves a witch horse!"

The men laughed, cold and cruel, while they led the girl with the white blonde hair and the horse with the scraggly grey coat towards the town, all too close. All the while, Fae looked backwards; backwards towards home where her mother lay on her deathbed. Backwards towards the direction in which her sisters had disappeared, leaving her all alone. And backwards towards the eerie black clouds galloping towards her like a death threat.

"The storm," she said. Her damp coat billowed, and around her, Fae's hair danced like ribbons in the wind. The snow was falling as sleet, big sloppy ice and water soaking her and the men and the horse.

"Shut up!" Boris said, giving her a shake for good measure. But Fae did not take her eyes from the clouds racing in the sky, though she tripped several times over stones under bare feet. The hooded man drew close, dragging the reluctant horse with him.

"Don't worry about the storm, my Darkness," he said to Fae, sickly sweet and all the more menacing for being so. "The town is just around the corner and you'll both be burnt at the stake long before the rain comes to smother your ashes."

But for all Fae's fragility, for all her whispers and soft words and delicate, gentle ways, she did not fear. For she had deeper thoughts, thoughts as powerful as the storm winds themselves.

It's all my fault, but at least this way, my innocent sisters are safe. My only fear now is trying to save the innocent horse.

And will you save me? White asked, hearing the girl speak in her mind for the first time.

But unlike Amara, Fae did not disbelieve the horse could hear her. She already knew she had a witch heart. She had known it all her life—felt it beat with nature; noticing how her moods changed with the seasons or the mossy ground beneath her feet. How the rocks spoke of ancient times and the wind sung of faraway legends. Yes, she always knew, though she had never before spoken the words. So when she admitted it, the truth, it felt right and soft and true.

Fae smiled a smile full of weakness, and strength, and uncertainty. *Yes,* she said in the mind of White. *I* will *somehow save you...and if I can save you, maybe I can also save myself. And Mother, if it's not too late.*

Her heart broke a little then, tearing down one side as she thought of her poor, ailed mother in a cold bed, hungry and dying—alone. But somehow, the tear in her heart made it stronger, made it beat with a new rhythm, and the rhythm was one of hope.

She rounded the corner, but immediately staggered backwards with the immensity of the town and the jeering people. She gasped, eyes widening at the already burning witch pyres, the crowd bustling to get a better view with pitchforks in their hands and hatred in their hearts. The air smelt of smoke and flame and sorrow. Ashes caught in Fae's throat.

"The witches cometh!" cried an elderly voice in the crowd, and Fae's hope shrunk and tangled into a knot of hopelessness.

12

BURN THE WITCH

*T*he crowd was hungry for a witch, Fae could sense it and so, too, could White. The timid horse took worried, stilted strides that matched Fae's scuffling steps.

Please, White begged in a whisper in Fae's mind. *Please no...*

Fae closed her eyes hoping it would stop her tears rolling down her face. It didn't, and instead they made trails down her soot-smeared skin. The horse's fear was heartbreaking; it mingled with Fae's own. She turned to the man dragging her forward.

"Please let the horse go, she was nothing but spooked. You cannot be so cruel as to send an innocent animal to trial."

"Shut up, witch," the hunchback snarled then

giggled, unable to keep the excitement from his voice. "'Ere, stand still, will you?" A command, not a question.

The hooded man shouldered his way through the throngs, and the crowd began parting for him in advance. They didn't need to see the face hidden behind his hood to be repelled. A darkness clung to him and people backed away with an unknown instinct.

Fae watched him approach a man on a raised wooden stage where the pyres smoldered. She took a backwards step, her heart fluttering in her chest like a trapped bird in a cage.

The hunchback shook her. "Stand still! You ain't going nowhere but on them there burning pyres."

"I..." she began but trailed off, in awe of the man on the stage. His presence reached out across the land, and it had nothing to do with the fine, fine clothes he wore, the tall pointed top hat, or silvery cane he used when walking—though no limp was evident. And walk he did now, towards Fae and White, cane slicing through the melting snow and tapping on the hard stone beneath. *Tap. Tap. Tap.* The hooded man trotted to keep up, despite his long legs.

Fae gulped.

White whickered softly.

"A witch *and* her horse, you say?" inquired the

Witch Hunter General, his voice as smooth and sharp as cut silk. He loomed over Fae, and pinched her chin between his thumb and forefinger, forcing her head to the left then to the right, inspecting her. He dropped his hand and glanced at the horse. "You are right. I do not need to trial either, I can tell by looking in their eyes. Darkness, through and through."

He smiled; chilling and warm, kind and terrible all mixed into one. Then he dug a slender, leather-clad hand into his pocket and fished out two gold coins, thrusting them into the hooded man's hand.

"Only two?" Boris questioned.

The Witch Hunter General cast him a look so fierce the hooded man shrank and said no more, pocketing both coins while the hunchback beside him stared open mouthed.

The Witch Hunter nodded to a woman Fae had not before noticed lingering at his side, and instantly the portly woman rang a bell she carried in her gnarled hand.

It clanged into the darkening sky, pounding to the tune of sadness and death. The villagers, the hustle and the bustle, silenced. And they turned, watching with fear and intrigue as the man with a cane flung his arms wide.

"Hear me, hear me!" he called out, his voice

bellowing like the echoes of the bell. "We have here not only a witch, but an animal she has cursed. Today, I save you all from *both* evils."

The crowd shuffled, agitation spiraling upwards towards the thunderous storm clouds forming in the east.

"I cast no vote," the man said. "I say guilty, guilty as charged!"

The crowd bellowed, "Burn the witch! Burn the witch!"

The old woman with the bell went about the townsfolk collecting coins in payment for this *great* deed. Nobody complained, digging deep into their superstitious pockets.

The stage was set. Fire and flame licked the sky, dancing on the wind, while cold, hard hands bustled both Fae and White toward the stage. Fae's hands and feet were bound, and the horse's legs hobbled as the crowd hollered and jeered, but Fae did nothing more than stare into those flames, watching them dance and curl and smolder. And somehow, the blazing heat reminded her of Morganne and her red, red curls and fiery, fierce protection. The black smoke swirling and curling into the air reminded Fae of Amara, of her seriousness, her depth, and changing tides. And the wind in which both flame and smoke danced, reminded

Fae of the flickering feeling she had deep inside. The power of the world, swirling around like a gale inside her stomach.

"Fear not, little horse," she said aloud. She looked skywards towards the blackening clouds racing towards her.

And she smiled.

13

UNDONE

"Faster, Black," Amara cried aloud, as the horse thundered across the ground. "We must go faster."

Thrumming hooves and heartbeats pounded, Black and Red neck and neck, stride for stride, flying with speed a horse had never before known. Ears flat back they continued racing toward the town and the spiraling black smoke from the witch pyres. They were already travelling with unnatural speed, and Amara found herself tiring with the use of such magic.

You must save some energy for yourself, Red warned once again. *Who knows what we'll discover when we get to the town.*

And how much magic you may need to save White and your sister, Black added. Neither horse seemed out of breath as they travelled in a whirl of frenzy and magic.

"Will we make it?" Morganne asked, shouting over the wind that whipped her words into the air. Her hair flailed around her pale face, chasing her like a flame, while her silken gown blazed and billowed.

Amara turned her head as they galloped on. "We must."

All around, snow melted, sleet pounded, but neither the girls nor the horses felt the slap of thawing ice on skin. They galloped, chasing the storm ahead of them, hoping it could reach Fae and the flames before it was too late.

Ropes tightened. Wood crackled. Heat shimmered in the cold, cold, air.

Fae cast a look towards the hooded man, his face unreadable—hidden in shadows and lies. Beside him, the hunchback raised a hand, and wiggled his big, thick fingers in a child-like gesture. The Witch Hunter General did not stop to watch, instead he loaded up his lavish carriage with large pots of gold, leaving his own henchmen to guard the stage.

Hundreds of eyes glared up at Fae and White; some full of fear and dread, others fixed in cold, hard stares of hatred.

"Fancy bewitching a poor horse," she heard an old woman mutter, then she spat at Fae's feet in disgust.

You have to do something, White said in Fae's mind. The horse writhed, trying to break the ropes, but her depleted body ached too much to make any difference. Instead, she trembled, her dirty grey coat soaked with heavy sleet.

Fae concentrated. There was one thing knowing she was a witch, but creating magic was, well, magical. It was different from *feeling* nature. She had to *become* it. She thought hard about freedom and the tight, tight knots pinning her and White to the stakes. And suddenly, the ropes began writhing.

"Yes!" Fae said. "I did it."

The ropes started to loosen.

A short-lived victory; as now, the thick ropes continued to writhe, but wrapped themselves tighter... and then they hissed.

White shrieked. *Snakes! Snakes!* The horse screamed, her tone one of terror and death. She scrambled on the spot, her hooves clattering against the wooden stage. The crowd gasped. Many scarpered.

"Burn the witch!" they screamed as they ran.

Fae whimpered. "What have I done?"

The hunchback staggered backwards. The hooded man laughed.

And several snakes coiled towards Fae's terrified face, mouths open, pointy tongues flicking.

Hooves clattered over the bridge and around the bend, slipping and sliding on the soaked ground, but not slowing.

"We're nearly there," called Amara, low and light on the horse's back, allowing Black to move freely underneath her. They clattered around another corner, banking hard to the left and Amara's midnight black gown caught and snagged on a stone jutting from wall. The dress tore but they pounded on.

White! screamed Red behind, as a terrified neigh echoed on the stone walls around them, a maze of alleyways and narrow streets.

Their speed quickened. Thunder grumbled. And Fae's scream chilled both Amara's and Morganne's bones.

"Oh! Our darling little sister," Morganne cried.

Amara's anger and panic flowed as tears; her body weak and exhausted. Above them, the black clouds opened, and torrential rain poured down like violent, cascading waterfalls.

Dozens of snakes writhed over White and Fae. The remaining crowd too stunned to move as they watched in awe and disgust. Then the rain came, heavy and pounding. The crowd scattered, covering their heads with their arms that offered no protection from the battering rain. Screaming and jeering and shouting amidst the otherworldly storm, they dispersed.

"Get to the inn, Cuthbert!" the hooded man yelled amidst the throng. Cuthbert stood, eyes wide with horror at the slithering snakes dancing around their sold cargo. "We have our gold, no need to stay now!"

They darted away. Rain continued to pelt, getting heavier and heavier, sizzling on the flickering flames, smoke choking Fae's lungs. But the men stopped as galloping hooves splashed in puddles ahead of them. And there, a vision emerged that nearly caused Fae's heart to burst with joy.

"Sisters!" Fae called, urgent as a whirlwind.

Red and Black stopped short, nostrils flared, their warm breath forming a white mist around them in the cold air. Their muscles rippled and glistened with sweat and... and something else. Power and magic and strength. Morganne and Amara hesitated, hands to mouths aboard their magnificent beasts, watching the writhing snakes.

"Get them," the hooded man yelled. "Get our triplets, and we'll get the gold we were promised."

The hunchback hesitated, then lumbered towards the sisters, hesitant. But neither Morganne nor Amara moved. They did not fear the hunchback, they feared a far bigger danger, and they watched, helpless, as a grotesquely large snake make its way towards Fae's pretty, pale face.

Rain seized the flames licking at Fae's toes, water over fire, but this did nothing to ease Fae's tremulous heart. She stared into the reptile's eyes, small ebony slits in amber flames—and held her breath.

The snake opened its mouth, fangs exposed, and it spoke, "Life for life," it hissed. And slowly, slithered past Fae's head to the wooden stake behind her, and slid away. Each snake followed in turn, from Fae, from White, hissing their thanks as they coiled and slithered toward the hooded man and the hunchback.

"What's this?" The hooded man yelled, enraged. Then, fearful. "Run Cuthbert, run!"

And away they lumbered, but they were no match

for the serpents. With two fierce hisses, and two sharp bites, the men fell to the soaked ground, slapping into puddles rippling with wind and rain.

Amara, exhausted, collapsed over Black's neck, breathing shallow. After several breaths, she forced herself to sit back up, and using the very last of her magical energy, Amara snapped her fingers—the rain ceased immediately.

Upon the stage, Fae smoothed White's trembling neck and closed her eyes. Returning the gesture, White rested her forehead against the witch's own, offering a deep thanks no words could express; a silence only understood by those lucky enough to win the love of a horse.

After several long heartbeats, Fae opened her eyes and turned to Amara. "How did you do that?" she asked, astonished, and held her hands aloft with wonder at the ceased rain. She descended the stage, too full of emotion to run to her sisters.

Amara, incredulous and despite her depleted energy, laughed. "And how did *you* do *that?*" she asked, pointing to the snakes.

"Dear sisters," Morganne said. Eldest. Voice of reason. She looked around at the sizzling pyres, the empty town square, their captors snoring heavily on the ground at their feet. Her two younger sisters: Amara;

middle sister, hair and heart of midnight skies. Fae; youngest sister, hair and heart of wind and light.

Witches both.

Morganne sighed, smiled, and said with the authority only owned by eldest sisters. "Let us go home."

14

NAMESAKE

*H*ours of joviality passed, where the three sisters simply enjoyed riding through the countryside toward home, recounting tales already full of flourishes destined to swell with each telling. Stories are like that.

Now, they remained silent, deep within their own thoughts. The only sound being the occasional soft snort from the horses, and swishing of tall lush grass, like an ocean shore breathing as their steeds strode through. The horses snatched at mouthfuls as they passed, and the sisters did nothing to stop them. They had long ago removed their bridles and were simply passengers, allowing the horses to taste the sweetness freedom brought.

"I've been thinking," Fae said, as soft as wind from a

butterfly's wing. And though she did not need to speak aloud for the horses to hear her, she did so to allow her eldest sister a chance to understand. "You should choose your names, your *real* names." With a tender touch, Fae smoothed White's sleek neck, now adorned with dapples and a silver mane glistening under the moonlight.

"Yes," Amara agreed, as serious as ever. "There is much power in a name."

The horses remained silent in thoughtful contemplation, as did Morganne, who tried not to allow jealousy to creep through her blood and out of her mouth. She looked over her shoulder to see her witch sisters riding single file behind her, and wished her heart to beat with the same song.

And they rode like this, under the pallid, waning moon, in single file—together and alone in their own deep thoughts. The landscape dwarfed them in its vastness, rolling hills, black on black against the nighttime sky. Morganne and Amara's gowns tumbled and trailed over their horses' strong rumps, grazing the floor; the fabric as rich and vibrant as the horses' cascading tails held high and proud. And the horses' coats glistened under the moon waning in the starlit sky. Only Fae decided against a gown, and instead wore her simple grey cloak. It somehow felt more like *her*, and she smiled as the landscape gave way to the old familiar woods surrounding their home village.

White broke the silence. *I think I know my name… Moonshine*, she said, feeling the words in her mind like an unfinished poem; the sentiment right, but the words not quite so. Above the travelers, the moon glowed silver, shining over the mare's coat making it a direct reflection of the moon's magical surface. *No*, White continued, sure now that she could wrap her words around the poem in her mind. *Moon*glow.

"Ah," sighed Fae, feeling the truth of it. "Moonglow. That is a grand name."

"And you?" Amara asked Black, who had been contemplating his true name his entire life. He knew who he was, deep inside; as wistful as the wind and as dark as shadows. Yes, he was both midnight and flight —the dark side of the moon as she rests.

Shadowind, he proclaimed, and he somehow grew into himself, tall and proud and knowing. Wind whistled through the trees, shivering leaves and tussling through his midnight black mane and tail. Yes. The wind agreed, and he reveled in the sensation.

Red hesitated.

"What's wrong," Amara asked, "do you not yet know your own namesake?"

"It's okay if you do not," added Fae. "It should feel right, and if not, then wait. It will come to you."

Red snorted. *It's not that,* he began. *It's that I feel sorry for Morganne, for she can not participate in the naming ceremony.*

Both sisters looked at their eldest with a flicker of sympathy, and Morganne scowled, turning away. Amara spoke aloud then, sharing Red's sentiments with her magic-less sister, and this softened the frost growing around Morganne's heart. She petted Red, feeling his soft warm coat beneath her midnight cold hands.

"You are an angel," she whispered to him, feeling his warmth swell, wrapping itself around her. "My angel fire."

Red cast a sudden neigh echoing into the night, making the sisters jump, the horses start, and a lone owl hoot above them in the trees.

That is it, Red proclaimed to the others, though Morganne could not hear. *That shall be my name. Angelfire. Tell her, tell her she chose.*

And Amara did, but gained nothing more than a flicker of a half smile from her sister. Amara tried to ignore her blood singing to the tune of 'something is wrong.'

15

HOMESTEAD

*M*organne remained silent, not hearing the horses, but deep in her own thoughts. She watched her sisters laugh and giggle and sigh with sweetness. They translated the horses' thoughts to her but it wasn't quite the same. Morganne didn't like to think it, but her heart hung heavy with longing. Longing to be with her sisters as she always had been. Longing to be what she feared all her life she would become—a witch.

"What will the horses do once they take us home?" Morganne asked her sisters. She bit down her jealousy when Amara and Fae went into silent and secret conversations. Conversations shared only by *special* ones.

We don't have to go, you know, said Angelfire, jigging a little with excitement. *I like to think we are all friends now.*

Yes, a shared adventure can do that.

"Well, you will be free to come and go as you please," Amara said. Serious. Stoic. And the horses whickered. "But there will always be a safe place and plenty of fodder for you with us. Our home is yours."

Home, said Shadowind. *That would be nice.* And his mind drifted off to long fresh grass and warm, comfortable stables as they meandered through a path in the woods so familiar to the sisters.

"Sister?" Amara asked, turning to Morganne and watching her sullen features contorting into an almost frown. "You are so quiet, won't you say what is bothering you?"

Amara was right, of course; she knew these things, especially when under an *almost* full moon. But she did not need magical powers to sense her sister's heavy heart.

There *was* something bothering Morganne, and she bit back her irritation, keeping her voice calm and even as she spoke. "If you always had a feeling you were witches, why keep it to yourselves? Why did you not trust in our sisterhood?" But silently, in her own private conversation, she asked another question. *Why did you not trust me?*

Amara smiled apologetically. "I did not want to believe it. I was afraid."

Fae looked away. "I thought you would both disown me."

They rode silently for a while. Thoughtful.

"Morganne?" Amara asked. "Do you not feel it? Not even a *little*?"

Morganne shook her head, red curls bouncing as she did so. She pulled up the hood of her glorious red cape to hide her face and stinging tears. "No, nothing at all. Never."

They rode on again, the horses' hoofbeats muffled by the soft forest loam and midnight stillness.

Morganne's face suddenly scrunched up, a realization. An anger.

"You know, *all* of this could have been prevented— getting captured, Mother on her deathbed—if you just believed in yourselves from the beginning," Morganne spat, annoyed and superior, like older sisters sometimes are. "You could have saved us from getting caught, or better yet, found the Witch Hazel to heal Mother in an instant."

Amara and Fae turned away; from Morganne, from the truth.

She was right. But Morganne didn't stop, she vented, angrier still, worried that they may not have a mother to go home to, worried their mother may be as cold and breathless as the still midnight air. "You could have found the herb to cure Mother just by clicking you fingers like so..." Morganne clicked her fingers to demonstrate, and instantly, the thick, green herb formed in her hand.

She gasped, staring at the herb and her hand in wonderment, awe, and a hint of fear. "I... *how?*"

Fae squealed with shrill laughter, light and airy enough to ward away Morganne's gloom. Amara smirked, a rare oddity.

"How?" she questioned again, any certainty usually belonging to eldest sisters disappearing as quickly as a snuffed candle flame. And perhaps she would have continued to question, but they had reached the end of the woods, and the gate at the bottom of their garden creaked open in welcome.

The horses came to a halt in a line, and the sisters of three stared at their home, then to each other. Even Amara smiled.

In the shadow of midnight, their cottage shone— warm and welcome orange light flickered from the windows. The smell of fresh bread wafted through the open kitchen window where Shadow sat on the squashed Chrysanthemums as though they were his throne.

"That cat!" Amara scowled happily with a shake of her head. Her ebony curls tumbled around her pale face as she watched Shadow jump down from his throne. The front door opened.

"What took you?" A welcome, chastising voice.

"Mother!" The three sisters called with delight as the portly woman rubbed flour from her hands onto her apron. Shadow curled in and out of her stocky legs.

"You're well!" cried Fae. She dismounted and ran to her as swift as an autumn breeze, blonde hair trailing from her grey cloak. "But... how?"

Mother cast a rueful smile, bent down, and bundled Shadow into her arms. He purred and rubbed his face into her own. "This little beast brought me some herbs..." She regarded her daughters and the aura of magic surrounded them before continuing, "...just like a good witch's cat should do."

Mother and daughters shared glances, then laughter.

Amara dismounted Shadowind, who instantly went wandering to graze, and Amara looked at the waning moon with a smile. Her heart sung a song, and she had a feeling that everything would be all right. And she should know. Amara always had her best ideas when staring up at the moon, even perhaps, if it wasn't *quite* full.

The door closed behind the witches and their mother while the horses rested on long, soft grass, and drifted off to sleep with the sound of clattering soup bowls and laughter drifting from the kitchen. In the woods, a lone wolf cried, but somehow, the sound was not one to fear.

Onwards, it seemed to sing to the waning moon.

Onwards.

Three Weeks Later...

*M*organne clicked her fingers time and time again, the pads of her first finger and thumb red raw. A knot of questions formed between her brows, and her pulse ticked at her sweating temples

"I don't understand..." she muttered again through gritted teeth. Morganne blew out a short, sharp breath, looking up at her sisters both and slapped her hands on the worn kitchen table. Fae gave an awkward smile when the plates upon the table clattered in protest. She had long ago given up on encouraging her eldest sister to perform magic.

Amara shuffled in her seat, feigning interest in

Shadowind as he frolicked in the distance beyond the window of the cottage.

"It's been three weeks and still, the only magic I have performed was summoning up the stupid herb, while your magic flourishes like flowers in spring," Morganne said with frustration and spite both.

"Sister," Fae said with the cool warmth and sadness of the last evening in summer. "Perhaps because you try too hard. You'll make yourself ill continuing in this manner. You're not eating, hardly sleeping. And your frustration is making you..."

"Making me what?" Morganne demanded. "Angry? Irritable? Desperately sad? You'd feel all these things too if it were I who glowed with magic along with our mother's precious Amara, while you attempted magic in vain." Morganne shot Amara a look that would have turned her younger sister to stone—were she able to use magic.

Morganne stood, her wooden stool clattering behind her on the cold flagstone floor. She pulled her wild red haired into a scruffy ponytail and strode from the darkening room.

"Morganne," Amara called, closing her eyes and holding her breath. Her sister continued striding away so Amara was forced to use her voice inside her sister's mind. *Morganne, it's not your fault.*

Silence. Amara squirmed in her seat. She hoped this moment would not come. She hoped her eldest sister's magic would grow, or at the very least start.

But it hadn't, and Amara could lie no longer. *It was I who summoned the herb into your hand, for I did not want you to feel left out...*

She felt Morganne's thunder before her elder sister streaked into the room like a bolt of fiery lightning.

"You did what?" Morganne cursed. She loomed over Amara in such a way that Fae ran over, putting herself between them. "Get out of my way, youngest sister."

Fae, confused, turned to Amara who rose— composed and steady as always; a flicker of her heavy-lashed eyelids the only thing that gave her apprehension away. "I assumed your magic was just slow in coming, I never suspected that your magic would not come at all."

"So you lied to me for weeks!" Morganne stormed away, pacing, fingers at her trembling lips. "You watched me try, hour after hour, day after day, for *three weeks* and all this time you knew it was impossible..."

"Is this true?" Fae asked, astonished.

Amara nodded once. "Though I did not believe it impossible—I thought your magic would come. I never suspected..." she trailed off, eyes downcast.

"How dare you," Morganne spat with a cool venom that had never before passed her lips. She stormed away, all heartache and fury.

And neither Amara nor Fae needed foresight to know that trouble loomed ahead...

End of Episode One

Find out how far Morganne is prepared to go to feel the touch of magic in Episode Two - Fire Heart...

https://books2read.com/u/brGRaY

FIRE HEART

"We blend our spells from fire and hell
To fill the moon with red.
Her blood will spill, the world will still,
Until the witch is dead."

Morganne is losing all hope of ever feeling magic surge through her veins. And all the while, her sisters' magic flourishes by the day. She will do anything for a witch heart so when she discovers a mysterious grimoire full of dark spells and darker promises, Morganne is compelled to learn its secrets.

But all magic comes with a price, and soon Morganne's seemingly innocent desire puts all she knows and loves in mortal danger, and opens a door into terrible secrets full of passion, madness, and revenge.

The price for knowledge is life—and somebody is going to have to pay...

THE STAKES ARE RAISED...

The battle between good and evil just got real... read the thrilling Magic and Mage sequel, FIRE HEART here: https://books2read.com/u/brGRaY

GET YOUR

Free Reader Swag Bag!

SIGN UP TO MAGIC AND MAGE READERS' COVEN NEWSLETTER & GET

Free
* Colouring Pages
* Printable Bookmark
* Character Interviews
* Monthly Updates!

Author Notes

I love interacting with readers, so why not download the free Swag Bag and join me in my newsletter space for more giveaways, special readers discounts, and more!

Come and join the Cool Club just here!

https://pages.convertkit.com/f4060ebc76/e72e28f7e6

ABOUT THE AUTHOR

Angharad Thompson Rees is a poet, comic scriptwriter, and author of both the MG fantasy Magic and Mage series, and the Magical Adventures & Pony Tales children's series. A former equine professional with over 15 years experience working with top-class horses, Angharad now incorporates her knowledge into her equine themed fantasy series, creating fast moving plots that gallop along at speed!

facebook.com/angharadthompsonrees

twitter.com/1angharad_rees

instagram.com/angharadthompsonrees

VIP READERS

As always, I want thank my VIP Reading Team, who help me so much with their ongoing encouragement and support. Thank you for cheerleading me on this journey—as always, you guys keep my inkwell filled!

In particular, I'd love to thank VIP Readers, Dorothy, Saundra, and Jane who helped Red, Black, and White discover their real names by winning the name game competition! Such fabulous names! Thank you!

VIP READERS – WITH THANKS

Della, Sha, Paula, Jo, Essie, Linda, Saray, Mary,

Martha, Kandice, Belle, Kim, Catherine, Jackie, Ulrike, Dorothy, Zarine, Aj, Georganne, Claire, Anne, Wendy, Peggy, Debra, Anne, Terry, Janet, Floria, Aryn, Elizabeth, Roeshell, Susan, Tamber Bliss, Jazz, Julia, Shauna, Hazel, Elsbeth, Lana, Carlynne, Aniket, Michelle, Jennifer, Brenda, Debbie, Saundra, Jane, Martina, Carol, Leanne, Debbie, Tiffany, Pam, Bruce, Shari, Emily, Clara, Laurel, Nancy, Scarolet, Heather, Becky, Marie, Kerry, Karin, Paul, Abigail, Carole, Linda, Tanya, Marc, Rita, Marilyn.

First published in 2018
by Little Whimsey Press

Cover Design by OliviaProDesigns
Editing by Phoenix Editing

Printed in Poland
by Amazon Fulfillment
Poland Sp. z o.o., Wrocław

56190680R10063